W9-BRM-457

Mrs. Armitage
and the
Big Wave

Quentin Blake

HARCOURT BRACE & COMPANY

San Diego   New York   London

For Ali and Laurie and Lucy

First published in the United Kingdom in 1997 by Jonathan Cape, Random House
First U.S. edition 1998

Library of Congress Cataloging-in-Publication Data
Blake, Quentin.
Mrs. Armitage and the big wave/Quentin Blake.
p. cm.
Summary: Mrs. Armitage and her dog Breakspear head out surfing,
but each time they paddle out they think of another outlandish thing they need.
ISBN 0-15-201642-2
[1. Surfing—Fiction. 2. Dogs—Fiction. 3. Humorous stories.] I. Title.
PZ7.B56Mp 1998
[E]—dc21 97-15420

A C E F D B

Printed in Hong Kong

Mrs. Armitage was on her way to the beach.
She was wearing her surfing gear and she
carried her surfboard under her arm.
Breakspear the dog ran alongside.

When they got to the beach, they walked
across the sand and into the water.

"What we have to do, Breakspear," said
Mrs. Armitage, "is swim out to sea and
wait for the Big Wave."

But while they were waiting for the
Big Wave, Mrs. Armitage could see that
Breakspear's little legs were getting tired.
"What we need here," said Mrs. Armitage,
"is something to keep a faithful dog afloat."

So she swam back to the beach and bought
an inflatable desert island.

When she got back, Breakspear climbed
onto the desert island and they went on
waiting for the Big Wave.

But it was a hot, hot day and soon
Mrs. Armitage was sweating and
Breakspear's tongue was hanging out.
"What we need here," said Mrs. Armitage,
"is something to protect us from the
sun's powerful rays."

So she swam off and came back with a cap
with a yellow plastic brim for herself and
an umbrella with pink spots for Breakspear;
and they went on waiting for the Big Wave.

Now they were nice and cool, but soon they began
to feel rather hungry, as one does at the beach.
"What we need here," said Mrs. Armitage,
"is a selection of light snacks to keep us going."

So she swam off and got a plastic duck and an
empty box, tied them together with string,
and filled the box with tasty items.

When she got back, Mrs. Armitage ate
an avocado burger and Breakspear had
some crunchy dog biscuits and they
went on waiting for the Big Wave.

After a while a breeze sprang up and blew
briskly along the shore.
"This is delightful," said Mrs. Armitage,
"but what we need here is something
to show us Wind Force and Direction."

So she swam off and came back with a wind sock and a string of flags, and she fixed them so that they blew in the breeze. Then Mrs. Armitage and Breakspear went on waiting for the Big Wave.

A wind surfer passed them at high speed.
"Hi there, gorgeous!" he shouted.
"What we need here," said Mrs. Armitage,
"is something we can hail fellow
sportsmen with."

So she swam off and came back with
a red megaphone. She brought a horn
as well because it's always a good thing
to have a horn.

Then she gave a few shouts and hoots
and they went on waiting for the Big Wave.

By now all kinds of fish were popping
their heads out of the water to find out
what the fuss was about.
"I hope there aren't any sharks,"
said Mrs. Armitage.
So she swam off . . .

. . . and came back with a sturdy boat hook.
"Now we can give a prod to any shark that
wants to bother us," said Mrs. Armitage,
and they went on waiting for the Big Wave.

And then the Big Wave came.
At the same moment, they noticed
a little girl named Miranda who had
swum out too far and was in trouble.

"Pah-hee-hah-hurgh," went Mrs. Armitage
on the horn. She hooked Miranda with
the boat hook and off they went.

They did a California slither,
    a Bali swerve,
        a Waikiki flip and . . .

. . . landed on the beach right in front
of Miranda's parents.

They all went to the beach café to celebrate.
"There's still time, Breakspear, for us
to have another go," said Mrs. Armitage.

"But what we *really* need is . . ."